Kids l[...] [...]
Choose You[...]

"These boo[...]
Sometimes the choice seems like it
will solve everything, but you wonder
if it's a trap."

Matt Harmon, age 11

"I think you'd call this a book for active
readers, and I am definitely an
active reader!"

Ava Kendrick, age 11

"You decide your own fate,
but your fate is still a surprise."

Chun Tao Lin, age 10

"Come on in this book if you're crazy
enough! One wrong move and
you're a goner!"

Ben Curley, age 9

"You can read *Choose Your Own
Adventure* books so many wonderful
ways. You could go find your dog
or follow a unicorn."

Celia Lawton, age 11

**Ask your bookseller for books you have missed
or visit us at cyoa.com to collect them all.**

CHOOSE YOUR OWN ADVENTURE® 37

PIRATE TREASURE OF THE ONYX DRAGON

BY ALISON GILLIGAN

ILLUSTRATED BY: GABHOR UTOMO

CHOOSECO
WAITSFIELD, VERMONT

Pirate Treasure of the Onyx Dragon ©1990 R. A. Montgomery,
Warren, Vermont. All Rights Reserved.
Originally published as *Treasure of the Onyx Dragon*

Artwork, design, and revised text ©2011 Chooseco LLC,
Waitsfield, Vermont. All Rights Reserved.

Illustrated by: Gabhor Utomo
Book design: Stacey Boyd, Big Eyedea Visual Design

For information regarding permission, write to:

CHOOSECO
P.O. Box 46
Waitsfield, Vermont 05673
www.cyoa.com

ISBN-10 1-933390-99-9
ISBN-13 978-1-933390-99-4

Published simultaneously in the United States and Canada

Printed in Canada

0 9 8 7 6 5 4 3 2 1

For David, Walker, & Penn

BEWARE and WARNING!

This book is different from other books.

You and YOU ALONE are in charge of what happens in this story.

There are dangers, choices, adventures, and consequences. YOU must use all of your numerous talents and much of your enormous intelligence. The wrong decision could end in disaster—even death. But, don't despair. At any time, YOU can go back and make another choice, alter the path of your story, and change its result.

The mysterious waters off San Juan Island may hold many surprises for you to explore. Even if you do locate the missing ship and its precious cargo, you won't necessarily be able to keep your treasure!

Good luck!

You and your younger sister, Hannah, spot your Aunt Lydia at Seattle Tacoma International Airport as you exit Customs. She is waving her handkerchief in your direction as she calls, "Oh, yoo-hoo! Here I am!"

Aunt Lydia is your father's older sister. During the school year you and Hannah live in Egypt. On weekends you work on archeological digs. Although you are young, your knowledge of Egyptian hieroglyphics is a valuable tool on these digs. Ever since your father disappeared on a dig several years ago, your aunt has insisted that you and Hannah spend your summers at the family house on San Juan Island. Dusty trenches in foreign countries during blazing hot summers are no place for you and your younger sister, she maintains.

While you're away on San Juan Island, your mother continues to work on the dig, thinking your aunt's invitation for the two of you to spend summers in a cooler climate is a splendid idea. Every time you return to the majestic beauty of the Pacific Northwest, you agree.

Turn to page 2.

2

Aunt Lydia commandeers a redcap for your luggage, and the three of you walk out into the bright sunshine. Whenever you see sun in Seattle you smile to yourself. Although it definitely rains in the Pacific Northwest, summers tend to be sunny and comfortably warm.

Lydia is a famous art historian, known around the world for her expertise in Asian art. Within your family she is known for being rather eccentric. She has a strange style of dressing. Today Aunt Lydia looks like she's heading off on safari— leather boots, a green linen skirt and jacket, a pith helmet, and a pointed walking stick. She is quite unusual, but she is also your favorite relative.

Last summer you found your father's high school diary at the bottom of an attic trunk. In it he wrote about his search for a treasure ship that sank off the coast of San Juan Island:

"Day 63 in my search for the sunken ship, the *Onyx Dragon*. Have told Lydia about my discovery of Great-Uncle MacGregor's letter. She seemed strangely upset and tried to warn me against continuing my search. As a precaution I have ripped the directions off the bottom of the letter and hidden them. I don't want any more of Lydia's pesky interference with my plans."

Go on to the next page.

According to the research you've done over the past year, the *Onyx Dragon* has never been found. You've spent hours trolling the Internet for ancient NW shipping routes, ship cargo manifests, and tales of unrecovered treasure and downed boats. You subscribe to an amazing wreck website, granting you access to maritime charts, wreck data, and a recovered artifact database. You've even discovered an obscure nautical archive that keeps records of violent storms and the ships they've claimed. The *Onyx Dragon* is prominently featured in the year 1852. All year long you've been planning to continue your father's search for the ship.

"Any chance we could look for that treasure ship, the *Onyx Dragon?*" you ask Aunt Lydia hopefully.

Turn to the next page.

4

For a moment your aunt looks stunned as she whisks you off to San Juan Island in her vintage 1969 Lamborghini Islero. "That ship has been down on the bottom of the sound for more than 130 years. If no one has found it yet, I doubt they ever will." She laughs darkly and presses her foot down on the accelerator.

Her car careens around corners. At times you swear that her vehicle is traveling on two wheels. You try to calm your nerves by making more conversation.

"Come on, Aunt Lydia. Tell me what you know about the sinking of the treasure ship!" you shout above the roar of the engine.

Aunt Lydia turns her steel-gray eyes on you. She slows enough for her voice to be heard. "The *Onyx Dragon* was loaded with precious cargo. Your Great-Great-Uncle MacGregor, the captain, was steering her through the Strait of Juan de Fuca."

The strait is the passageway from the ocean to Puget Sound, and it's peppered with over 400 islands, less than half of which are visible at high tide.

She pauses and stares into the distance. "The year was 1852. The ship broke up and sank during a fierce storm. For years, explorers from all over the world have been searching for the *Onyx Dragon*'s treasure—without any luck." She pauses for a moment. "That's all I know."

Your gut tells you she's hiding something.

Turn to page 7.

Strange, you think. Your father's diary made it sound like Aunt Lydia knew a whole lot more. *Sometime this summer*, you vow to yourself, *I'm going to find out what she's hiding and why.*

Hannah looks at you, her flaming red hair whipping in the wind. Her eyes twinkle mischievously. "That ship's just waiting for us to discover it," she whispers.

After another hour of Aunt Lydia's Formula One driving and one tranquil ferry ride later, the family's enormous Victorian summer home—which Aunt Lydia now holds the title to—stands before you. It's three stories high with lots of gables, turrets, and gingerbread trim. It sits on a bluff overlooking the churning water below. A small boathouse is nestled in a grove of madrona trees at the shore.

"I just love this house!" Hannah exclaims, jumping out of the car. "It's so beautiful and big, you could get lost in it."

"Sometimes," Aunt Lydia muses mysteriously, "without even trying."

Turn to the next page.

8

The house seems to hold many mysteries and memories. Wandering through its vast rooms, you feel closer to your father, knowing he spent his childhood summers here. Once again you feel a sharp hollow in your chest, the way you always feel when you realize how much you miss him.

On the fifth day of your visit, while exploring the house with Hannah, you lean against a giant urn in your grandfather's study. Suddenly the wall next to the urn silently swings open, revealing a short, dark passageway. Hannah races down the passageway. You quickly follow.

The passageway leads to a small room with leather-covered walls. It looks as if nothing in the room has been touched for years. Glancing around, you see shelves of old books, a large oak desk covered with dust, an ancient navigational telescope propped against the wall, and an enormous mirror in an ornate, gilded frame.

"This looks like a secret study," Hannah says.

One small window looks out over the bay. Furious waves smash against the black rocks below.

You run your hand along the mirror's trim, admiring the gilt frame. Suddenly it slips off the wall and crashes to the floor.

"Oh, no!" Hannah wails. "Seven years of bad luck!"

Go on to the next page.

You pick up the shards of glass, and crawl under the desk to get a large piece. You bump your head on the bottom of the desk. Just as you're about to howl out in pain, you look up. "Wow!" you cry. "Look what I just found." Hannah crawls next to you for a better look.

Two sheets of tea-colored paper are pinned to the bottom of the desk, you discover. You unpin the papers, crawl out, and spread them out on the floor.

"Look at all these weird arrows and signs," Hannah says. "This looks like it's written in some ancient language."

"Hardly," you reply with a certain smugness. "It's just written backward. Look." You hold up a piece of mirror and begin translating the writer's words.

"Listen to this," you begin excitedly.

"Dearest Miriah, I am writing this on my deathbed. There is a family secret that has haunted me for a long time. I will not take it to my grave! It has to do with our brother MacGregor's ship, the *Onyx Dragon*. On a cold blustery eve in 1852, his vessel had nearly reached its final destination: Seattle. The trip from Shanghai, China had been rough and difficult, and MacGregor was anxious as the ship was carrying a large cache of precious stones and gold—as well as the infamous emerald, the Star of Asia. The treasures had been recovered from the infamous pirate Lucy Morel, whose craft the Compass Rose had been discovered a week earlier in the trip, capsized and sinking.

Turn to the next page.

"As MacGregor steered the ship through the Strait of Juan de Fuca, a fierce storm blew down from the north. The Onyx Dragon was wrecked in the storm, and everyone on board drowned. The ship was thought to have run aground near—"

The remainder of the first page has been torn off.

"Hannah, do you know what this is?" you say excitedly. "This is the letter Dad discovered while searching for the ship. The bottom's ripped off just like he wrote in his diary."

"Who wrote the letter?" Hannah asks quickly. "And who is Miriah?"

"Let's see," you say, thumbing through the pages of your father's diary that you keep with you at all times. "According to the family tree Dad drew, Miriah was MacGregor's baby sister. She was only two years old when he died in the shipwreck. That means the letter must have been written by MacGregor's twin brother, Sean."

Go on to the next page.

"Read the second page of the letter!" Hannah says eagerly.

"Well, there appear to be three clues." You read aloud:

"There is a map hidden beneath the boathouse near the madrona tree. It was thrown in a bottle from the ship moments before the *Onyx Dragon* sank.

"Find the Indian, Mountain Spirit. He witnessed the sinking of the *Onyx Dragon* from high atop Mount Dallas. He can show you where the ship went down.

"Watch for mysterious lights in the night sky every year on the anniversary of the ship's sinking. Discover what they mean, and the treasure will be yours.

This is the break we've been waiting for!" you say.

"Which clue should we start with?" Hannah asks.

If you decide to search for the map beneath the boathouse, turn to page 12.

If you decide to begin by searching for Mountain Spirit's descendants, turn to page 20.

If you choose to pursue the mysterious lights, turn to page 24.

12

"I think the map beneath the boathouse holds the most promise," you say.

"Let's go!" Hannah agrees.

The two of you scramble out of the study and head toward your Aunt Lydia's gardening shed. You gather two shovels, a hoe, and hand trowels. At the last moment Hannah grabs the sonic beam detector. "Aunt Lydia showed me this yesterday," she says. "It's essentially a super-sophisticated metal detectors that uses ultrasonic waves to bounce off materials. It can penetrate anything."

You hide everything near the madrona tree at the base of the dock.

That night you sneak out, and the two of you scrape away at the dark earth around the tree by the glow of a full moon, hoping to locate the map. You poke the sonic beam's probes in and out of the tree roots. You see all kinds of rocks and even what looks like a rabbit's warren but nothing that looks like it might contain your map.

A large blister forms on the palm of your hand. "If I lift this one more time," you moan, "I swear my hands will fall off!"

"Let's call it a night," Hannah says, wiping sweat from her brow.

Once inside your room, you fall into bed without changing out of your clothes. In a matter of seconds you are in a deep sleep, dreaming about your Great-Great-Uncle MacGregor and the *Onyx Dragon*. MacGregor stands on the deck, trying to maintain his balance as the boat is pitched back

Go on to the next page.

and forth in a violent storm. Over the roar of the howling wind, you hear him calling your name. As you weave your way toward him, you realize he is pointing at the center of the boat. "Look there," he yells, "look there!"

You feel lost and confused. MacGregor now appears to be pointing to Aunt Lydia's boathouse, shining in the moonlight. "The rocks," he whispers, his voice growing faint as you strain to listen. "The rocks…" You are blinded by a glaring white light.

"My, oh my," your Aunt Lydia says, yanking back the curtains and allowing the bright morning sunshine to flood your room. "Whatever were you doing last night? Your clothes are covered with dirt, and you slept on top of the quilt." Smiling, she shakes her head and warns that if you don't wash and get dressed in a hurry, you'll miss out on her famous blueberry pancakes.

After breakfast you tell Hannah about your dream. For a moment her brow is furrowed in concentration. Then her eyes twinkle brightly with excitement. "Of course!" she whispers excitedly. "Our Uncle MacGregor was trying to give you a clue about the treasure map. When he pointed at the center of the ship he didn't mean the ship—he meant the boathouse!"

"That's obvious," you reply. Hannah is such a know-it-all. "But what rocks was he talking about? The ones his ship was about to strike, or…I've got it! He must have meant the rock wall behind the madrona tree!"

Turn to the next page.

14

Together you race toward the boathouse. Completely ignoring the pain from your blister, you break up the stone wall, shoving the rocks aside while Hannah shoves the sonic beam detector into the wet ground beneath.

At first the dark green LED screen shows a jumble of rocks, roots, and porous concrete. Slowly, however, the distinctive shape of an old bottle appears on the screen. You both pick up the pace of your digging.

Go on to the next page.

Within minutes your shovel clangs against a glass bottle. "This is it!" you yell, lifting the green glass bottle out of the ground.

Carefully you twist the cork out of the bottle. Inside is a tightly rolled piece of rough parchment, which you pull out slowly, careful not to let it tear. Unrolling the paper, you begin to examine its markings.

"It's the map!" Hannah says, clapping her hands.

"See this 'X' here," you say, pointing to a corner of the wrinkled paper. "I bet that's where the ship sank—and where the treasure lies, waiting to be discovered!"

"You're right!" Hannah says. "If we hurry we can catch Aunt Lydia's friend Zoot down at his dive shop before it closes for lunch. We'll need lots of gear and air tanks. We can stow everything in Aunt Lydia's boat overnight and take off at the crack of dawn tomorrow."

Turn to the next page.

16

Zoot is more than willing to rent you scuba gear at a discount price. "After all, you two were my best scuba diving students last year," he says cheerfully. Because of the cold water in Puget Sound, he helps you choose rubber pyrostretch neoprene jumpsuits and boots, Atomic dive rigging with eccoair tanks and flex hoses, compasses, headlamps, split fins, subframe masks, titanium knives, weight belts, guidelines—the list goes on for quite a while.

"I'll throw in two underwater slates for free," Zoot says kindly. "That way you can communicate below surface."

"We better get a couple of these as well," you say excitedly, holding up two goodie bags that you hope to fill with treasure.

Zoot eyes your haul with a twinkle in his eye. "If I didn't know better," he says, "I'd think the two of you had discovered a pirate's bounty!"

Turn to page 18.

18

Early the next morning, before anyone is awake, you jot a quick note to your aunt.

Hannah and I have gone out in the boat for the day. Back by dinner.

"The less we tell her, the better," you whisper. Hannah nods in agreement.

You take the helm of the boat and quietly glide out into the calm, misty waters of Haro Strait. The morning air is crisp and cool. Using local islands as your landmarks, you navigate to the area where the map indicates the *Onyx Dragon* sank. You pass Snug Harbor, Dead Man's Cove, and False Bay before heading south toward Ooger Island. Tall conifers rise dramatically from its rocky shores.

Hannah lowers the anchor. You struggle to climb into your diving gear. The rubberized material of the neoprene jumpsuit clings to your body like a second skin, and it takes a moment to adjust to its claustrophobic feeling. The early morning water looks dark and dangerous.

You look through the gear stowed in the ship's bow, searching for the deepwater headlamps. Not only do you find the lamps, you also discover an FJ3ZX—a sophisticated underwater echo probe.

"Look," you say, holding it up for inspection. "This is just what we need. It scans the bottom of the ocean using sound waves to identify objects and distances."

"The person who invented this probe became really famous," Hannah says with excitement. "Maybe we'll have the same luck."

Go on to the next page.

You read the instruction manual, then activate the probe and wait as it sends sound waves toward the bottom of the strait. As the waves head downward, they surround anything in their path, gauging the object's overall depth and shape. This information is then transmitted back to a small LED monitor on board, showing an outline on the screen.

You pull up the boat's anchor and begin drifting with the tides. Together you and Hannah spend the day scanning the ocean bottom, searching for the *Onyx Dragon*. Suddenly, on the screen, small objects appear scattered in a group over the ocean floor. Next to them is a large mass embedded in the sand. "The ship's hull!" Hannah yells in your ear.

You turn to tell your sister to lower her voice, but the sun setting against the Olympic Mountains makes you stop. "Let's dive for it now," Hannah says impatiently. "We can camp on Ooger Island tonight if we need to."

In a matter of minutes it will be dark. Night diving is dangerous. You know you promised Aunt Lydia you'd return by dinner, but the images on the sonic probe's screen make you hesitate. Should you risk an evening dive and spend the night camping on Ooger Island? Or should you return to Aunt Lydia's and resume your search tomorrow?

If you choose to head back toward shore, turn to page 29.

If you decide to dive now, turn to page 47.

Since American Indian folklore is one of your passions, exploring Mountain Spirit's sighting is too tempting to pass up. "Let's head over to the town library to do a little research," you say to Hannah.

The library is a sleepy, dusty old place that smells of shaved wood and glue. Just as you guessed, there is a section filled with volumes on local history and genealogies of native people and early settlers. Mrs. Cotier, the librarian, pulls a local historian's journal from the stacks for you.

"Just listen to this," you tell your sister as you pore over the journal.

> "It seems the Indian tribe living on Mount Dallas in 1852 were the Coast Salish. They were known among Indians throughout the country as fish-eaters because they ate so much salmon. They were also keen hunters of white-tailed deer."

"What about Mountain Spirit?" Hannah asks impatiently. "Does it say anything about his sighting?"

"Hold your horses," you answer, scanning ahead. "No, nothing. Although there is a chapter on shipwrecks in the islands. There's even a hand-drawn map with a bunch of 'Xs' to mark where boats went down.

Go on to the next page.

"Look—it mentions the *Onyx Dragon* here," you say, pointing to a page. "There's even a list of the treasure that went down with the ship.

> The ship's cargo hold was loaded with treasures that had been recouped from the pirate vessel the *Compass Rose*. Diamonds, rubies, and the largest emerald ever discovered, the Star of Asia, was believed to be on board.

Maybe Mrs. Cotier knows something about Mountain Spirit."

"Doesn't ring any bells," Mrs. Cotier says in answer to your question. "But the Coast Salish still live on a reservation here on San Juan Island. If I were you, I'd pay them a visit. Indians are great historians. I'm sure they could answer your questions."

"I think we should see if we can find more about the pirate ship," Hannah says. "That's got to be an important clue!"

To research the Compass Rose, *turn to page 23.*

To visit the Coast Salish Reservation, turn to page 35.

"It doesn't seem like the library will have information about the *Compass Rose*," Hannah says. "I think we should look on the Internet."

You let Hannah lead the search and within minutes, she's brought up a sketch of a young woman in pirate garb.

"The infamous Lucy Morel," Hannah reads, "one of the few female pirates of the nineteenth century, whose mysterious death in 1852 remained a part of pirate lore forever after. Although evidence of the *Compass Rose* sinking that year in the Indian Ocean has been verified by many, the treasures aboard the ship were never recovered, although the ship itself has been searched and remains mostly intact.

"What has caused suspicion among many who followed the story were that several of the gems Lucy had in her possession have resurfaced in the marketplace. Sightings of Lucy, whose body was never recovered, were reported in Thailand, France, and even the United States. There were even rumors of a romance with a US Navy Captain. But nothing was ever confirmed, and Lucy's mystery went with her to her grave—be it landlocked or oceanic, history may never know."

Hannah looks at you excitedly.

"Do you think her romance was with Great-Great-Uncle MacGregor?"

"I think it's time to visit Zoot at the scuba shop," says Hannah. "I want to start diving!"

Turn to page 16.

"The anniversary of the sinking is coming up. I don't see how we can pass up the chance to investigate the mysterious lights," you say. "Even Dad mentioned them in his diary."

You pick up the diary and read out loud,

> "Have heard old Belgrade down at the ferry talk about the lights on the anniversary of the *Onyx Dragon's* demise. Last year a fierce storm prevented me from venturing out to see them. This year, nothing can stop me."

"Did he see them that year?" Hannah asks.

"I don't know," you reply. "He stopped writing in his diary two days before the anniversary. I think maybe we should do a little more snooping around in here. Maybe we'll find some more clues."

You and Hannah spend the next few days hunting through your great-great-uncle's study. So far you've looked through all the desk drawers and bookshelves and found nothing.

Go on to the next page.

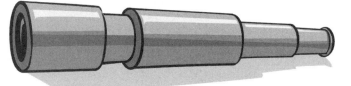

"One last look around and then let's quit," Hannah says. "The anniversary of the sinking of the *Onyx Dragon* is only three days away."

"Okay, okay," you reply, glancing around. "Now, let's see. If I were going to hide something in this room I'd put it in—there!" You leap toward the nautical telescope.

Removing the leather lens cap of the telescope, you peer inside. "I found it!" you cry.

You pull out a wrinkled, yellowed newspaper article from <u>The Seattle Post Intelligencer</u>. "Listen to this," you say with excitement.

Turn to the next page.

"June 27, 1855: There is a mystery brewing in Paris this summer that has set many tongues a waggin'. It seems that none other than Miss Daisy Dumas was spotted at the opera the other night wearing a large diamond brooch shaped like a dragon. What makes this story so intriguing is that the brooch was supposedly one of the treasures of the *Onyx Dragon* that sank off the Northwest coast of Washington, a mere three summers ago. Could it be that part of the elusive treasure has been discovered and sold without anyone knowing? This is a mystery indeed!"

"What does it mean?" Hannah asks.

"I don't know," you reply. "But I bet Aunt Lydia might." You head out of the study to find your aunt. She's in her flower garden, pruning roses.

"Hello, you two!" she merrily sings out. "Aren't these roses beauties?"

"Not bad," you say, barely glancing at the flowers. "Tell us more about the *Onyx Dragon*, Aunt Lydia."

Turn to page 28.

Aunt Lydia turns and stares at you, blinking rapidly. "I already told you everything I know," she says in a serious tone. "There's nothing more to say, really."

"Well, according to Dad's diary, there's a lot more," you say. "For instance, why didn't you mention the letter to Miriah that Dad told you about?"

Aunt Lydia's face turns ashen. "I'd—I'd forgotten about it," she says. "Besides, you two would be better off leaving certain stones unturned, if you know what I mean." She marches off, pruning scissors in hand.

"Aunt Lydia's acting kind of weird," Hannah says.

"Maybe it's just the old family memories," you say quietly. "Oh well. We'd better start planning for the anniversary. I want to be right there if those lights appear."

Finally the anniversary of the sinking of the *Onyx Dragon* arrives. After breakfast that morning Aunt Lydia calls you into her study.

"I have to go to the East Coast for a few days," she says. "The Metropolitan Museum of Art in New York wants me to authenticate a Chinese scroll before they purchase it. I'll be back before you know it." She smiles at you and goes upstairs to pack.

At dusk that evening, after Aunt Lydia has left, you and Hannah load up Aunt Lydia's motorboat with blankets and food and head out into Haro Strait. From your research you know the general area where the ship sank. You anchor your boat near Deadman's Bay and wait for something to happen.

Turn to page 73.

"It's too risky to dive now," you say to Hannah, turning the boat back toward San Juan Island. "We'll come back first thing tomorrow. The *Onyx Dragon* has sat on the ocean floor for over 160 years. She isn't going anywhere."

Back in the house, unable to keep your good news to yourselves, you excitedly tell Aunt Lydia about your discovery of the ship's location. You can tell she is nervous and upset.

"I thought you dropped the idea of searching for that treasure ship," she says sharply "You two don't know the Straits as well as I do. These waters can be very dangerous. Just think about the fate of the *Onyx Dragon* for a moment—the same thing could happen to you."

Seeing your frightened faces, her tone begins to soften. "Morning is only a few hours away. Get some sleep. We'll talk about it tomorrow." She smiles weakly as she leaves the room.

You and Hannah trudge upstairs to bed, mystified by your aunt's lack of enthusiasm. After tossing and turning for an hour or so, you whisper hoarsely to Hannah, "I don't know about you, Hannah, but I can't wait for morning. Let's go back out now, before Aunt Lydia has a chance to say no."

Turn to the next page.

"I'm with you," Hannah whispers back. Without another word, the two of you silently creep down the back staircase and open the screen door, pushing against its wood frame to prevent its ever-present squeak from announcing your departure. Quietly you and Hannah head off toward the boat moored at the dock.

You're out on the water for only a short time before a fierce storm blows down from the north.

"This is probably just like the storm that sank the *Onyx Dragon!*" Hannah yells above the howling wind. Your heart is pounding against your chest. With sweaty palms, you steer the boat toward a rocky island in the middle of the strait.

Turn to page 32.

The wind picks up, screaming past your ears. The driving rain stings as it slashes across your face. As you approach the island, Hannah spots a dark cave promising shelter. "Let's head for it," she yells over the din of the storm.

An eerie, bluish green light comes from within the cave's depths. It seems to bounce off the rock walls. Your boat drifts farther and farther into the cave's winding maze of canals, as if it were being drawn to the light.

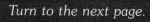

Turn to the next page.

34

The walls of the cave are glossy black. Water drips off the sharp stalactites hanging precariously overhead.

The closer you get to the light, the farther it drifts away. Intrigued, you follow the light deeper and deeper into the cave—before long you realize you are completely lost.

"Something about this cave gives me the creeps," Hannah says with a shiver. "Let's go back to the opening and wait out the storm."

"I hope you remember the way," you reply, "because I don't. We never set the guidelines. Besides, don't you want to find out where this light is coming from?"

Hannah grimaces and looks toward the dark depths of the cave in fear.

If you decide to find your way back to the cave's opening, turn to page 49.

If you choose to follow the eerie light, turn to page 53.

You copy the map from the journal onto a scrap of paper and head for home. After getting Aunt Lydia's permission, you pack your gear for an overnight visit to Mount Dallas. "Just remember," Aunt Lydia tells you as you head out the back door, "the Coast Salish are a very proud people. But they've fallen on hard times. Be respectful of their property and their customs."

You lead the way. At over 331 meters above sea level, Mount Dallas is San Juan Island's highest peak. After three hours of tough hiking, you're surprised you haven't reached the top.

"I sure could use a break," Hannah announces, leaning her backpack against a fir tree. "I could also use some lunch."

Once you've wolfed down two peanut butter and banana sandwiches, you feel rejuvenated. You start up the path ahead of your sister, but then you hear her calling your name.

Turn to page 37.

"What now?" you call back, turning around.

Hannah stands next to a boy dressed in a tee shirt and jeans. You scurry back down the path to find out who he is.

"This is Nootka," Hannah proudly tells you. "He's a member of the Coast Salish tribe."

Nootka is about your height and size. His face is deeply tanned. Around his neck is a leather necklace with four animal teeth. His large, dark eyes probe yours. For a moment you are frightened of his intense gaze. Pointing to the teeth on his necklace, you ask, "White-tailed deer?"

Turn to the next page.

Nootka's face breaks into a smile. "You bet," he says. "These are from my great-grandfather. I wear them for good luck when I'm farming my oyster bed. They came in handy today." He holds up a burlap sack filled with rough oyster shells. "Westcott Bay Petites. The best!"

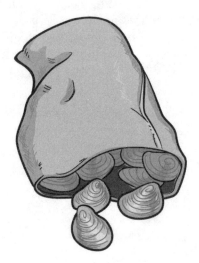

Quickly you explain your search for the story of Mountain Spirit's sighting. Nootka's knowing smile puts you at ease. "That's a famous tribal tale," he says proudly. "It's funny you should know about it, though. I didn't think it was repeated off the reservation."

He pauses for a moment. "I'll tell you what. I'll bring you home and introduce you to our tribal chief. You can ask him about the story. But I have to warn you," Nootka says cautiously, "I wouldn't be too hopeful. The tale is thought to be sacred. Usually it's only told during special ceremonies— and hardly ever to non-Indians."

With that, Nootka leads the way, deftly cutting through the forest at a quick pace. It is a struggle for you to keep up.

Half an hour later you find yourself at the Coast Salish reservation. Concrete and corrugated tin shacks surround a large stone building. From your knowledge of Indian customs, you know this is the longhouse, or ceremonial gathering place. Dense wood smoke seeps from a metal pipe in the center of the roof. Several small children play nearby in a clearing.

Turn to the next page.

40

To your left are four tall totem poles, beautifully carved and painted. The elegance of the totem poles gives a spiritual aura to the surrounding village. "This is home," Nootka tells you quietly. "And this is Nahpee, our tribal leader."

You turn around. Behind you stands an enormous man. He is dressed in an embroidered white shirt and jeans, and his long, black hair is pulled back into a thick braid. Around his neck is a necklace made up of many different sized teeth—*probably wolf or bear,* you think to yourself.

The tribal leader watches you in silence, listening to Nootka explain how he met you, your knowledge of Mountain Spirit's tale, and your request to hear it repeated. At the last suggestion, Nahpee's eyes squint at you suspiciously.

Turn to page 42.

"Why do you want to hear the tale?" he asks. His voice is so deep you can feel it vibrate in your chest. "Many people have asked to hear the tale. They pretended to be interested for historical reasons, but they were only after the treasure. Is that what you've come for?"

You feel as if Nahpee can read your mind. Afraid to lie, you reply, "Yes—and no. I mean, we'd like to find the ship, but mainly for personal reasons. You see, my Great-Great-Uncle MacGregor was the captain of the *Onyx Dragon* when it went down in the storm. My father searched for the ship when he was young. My sister and I are continuing his search."

Go on to the next page.

"And what of the treasure on board?" Nahpee asks. "Aren't you after that as well?"

"The treasure is secondary," you answer with sincerity. "Whatever we find we'd be happy to split with you—if you'll tell us the tale."

He stares at you intently, his coal black eyes focused in concentration.

"Perhaps you two are different from the others. I am not sure," Nahpee finally replies. "Stay for the night. We will consult our ancestral spirits for guidance and let you know their answer."

That night you gather outside the longhouse for a ceremonial dinner. Nootka and his family help prepare the meal over a wood fire. Several large salmon fillets are speared with sticks and propped next to the fire to smoke. Nootka places his oysters on a metal screen that is lowered over the red and orange flames. The heat from the fire steams open their shells. You and Hannah eat the meal in the traditional Salish way, dipping your food into carved bowls of fish oil. Everything is delicious.

"We have fish oil only on special occasions," Nootka whispers to you. "To our ancestors it was a valuable trade commodity and an indicator of wealth. It was often given at potlatches—ceremonial affairs where different tribes used to gather to exchange gifts and display their status."

Turn to the next page.

After dinner, six dancers link arms and slowly circle the fire. You are mesmerized by their movements. Nootka explains, "This is a transformation dance. The dancers ask the earth to provide an element to transform and reach out to our ancestors. You're about to see something amazing if the Earth agrees to their request."

You see a sudden tornado-like whirl of fog sweeping up the mountainside. The fog curls around the dancers' feet, moving faster and faster, higher and higher, until it completely surrounds them in a hazy mist. Just as suddenly it disappears, vaporizing into the night sky.

The dancers stop and huddle silently together, breathing deeply. After a few moments, the lead dancer approaches Nahpee and speaks in a hushed tone.

Nahpee turns to face the tribe. His voice is deep, rich, and proud. "Our ancestral spirits have spoken," he says. "Mountain Spirit trusts these children. He believes they come with good intentions. Their promise of half the treasure in exchange for the telling of the tale is made in good faith. Our whole tribe will benefit. The tale will be told."

You and Hannah sit in rapt attention as Mountain Spirit's sighting is retold through dances, songs, and the drawing of a map in the fire's hot ashes. When the evening is over you thank Nahpee and the whole tribe for the rare privilege of hearing the tale. Then you and Hannah retire to your tent, exhausted.

In the morning, when you compare the map from the historian's journal with the one drawn in the ashes, you're puzzled. The maps are similar in design, but the spot where the ship is supposed to have sunk is completely different.

"I'm not sure which map to trust," you say to Hannah.

"Beats me," Hannah replies.

If you decide to follow the instructions on the historian's map, turn to page 85.

If you decide to trust the Indian tale and the map drawn in the ashes, turn to page 89.

It takes you only a moment to think it over. "You're right, Hannah. We didn't come all this way to stop searching for the treasure once we found the ship." Your sister smiles in agreement.

Together the two of you wiggle into your neoprene suits. The rubber material sticks to your damp skin like glue. You strap on oxygen tanks, headlamps, and regulators, and jump overboard.

You signal to Hannah to wait while you tread water near the surface, your eyes adjusting to the darkness. Then, taking several deep breaths for courage, you propel yourself toward the bottom.

The water is cold and dark. A school of silver-colored fish swims by, causing you to gasp in fright. *This is silly,* you tell yourself. *In the daytime those fish wouldn't even make me flinch.*

Using your underwater compass, you head toward the mass you detected on the echo probe. Near the bottom, Hannah points to a small, shiny object half-buried in the sand. She digs it out and after a quick inspection excitedly points toward the surface.

"Up!" she writes on her underwater slate. "Treasure?"

Turn to the next page.

48

Back in the boat you inspect the object under your headlamps. It's a gold coin bearing the imprint of an ancient Chinese ruler.

"We found the treasure! We found it!" she yells. "We're right on top of it."

"Hold on," you say cautiously. "We may have found it, but it's too dark to search any longer." Hannah reluctantly agrees to head toward Ooger Island to set up camp.

Later, well fed and your tent up, you are ready to turn in. "I'll just check on the boat. Be right back," you say.

The shadow of a small ship, not far from shore, catches your eye. After a few moments you decide it's nothing more than a fishing boat and head back toward camp. *Odd*, you think, *that boat had no lights.*

Turn to page 54.

Cool, slimy beads of water drip onto your head and down your back. You can feel the hair on your arms stand up.

"Maybe you're right, Hannah," you say quietly. "Maybe we should go back. This cave can't be all that deep," you say, gently turning the boat around.

But as you steer back through the canals, you realize that you've lost your sense of direction. You have no idea how to locate the opening of the cave.

Every twenty yards or so you seem to come to a divide with two or three canals heading off into different directions. Despite your choices you feel like you're going around and around in circles—or worse, deeper and deeper into the dark cave.

Turn to the next page.

50

You lose all track of time. The clammy dampness of your skin makes you realize you've been circling for hours. It makes no difference in which direction you head. You seem to always wind up where you started. Hannah tries to remain calm, but you can feel her hysteria building.

You steer into a large lagoon. For a second you think you hear the wind howling. Suddenly something furry swoops down from above and brushes against your cheek. Hannah screams in terror. Thousands of bats whirl over your head, forming a funnel as they fly through the cave.

The bats race ahead of you. No doubt they are heading out into the night sky, you realize. In a cold sweat, you push the boat's throttle forward. But even at full speed your boat moves too slowly to keep up.

"If we lose sight of the bats, we'll never find the opening!" you cry in despair.

The flurry of bats slows to a trickle and then to a stop. The boat's motor makes a funny choking sound, coughs twice, and dies. An eerie silence fills the dark hollows of the cave. Your boat drifts aimlessly.

Hannah begins to whimper in the dark. The only other sound you hear is your heart, beating furiously against your chest. A slow terror begins to grow in the pit of your stomach. With a frightening certainty, you realize you will never find your way back to San Juan Island.

The End

Your curiosity about your aunt—who is supposed to be on her way to New York—gets the better of you. "Let's follow Aunt Lydia!" you say to Hannah. "It looks like she's going to Blakely Island."

You come about and follow Aunt Lydia's boat toward the island. She steers into a small cove, lands her boat on a rocky beach, and strides toward a wooden lean-to. A twelve-foot speedboat is anchored near the shore.

"Cut the engine and pull into the next inlet," Hannah says. "We can backtrack through the woods. It looks like she's going to meet someone in that shelter."

You tie your boat to a large fir tree in an inlet down shore. As quietly as possible, you and Hannah creep back through the dark woods. Soft pine needles blanket the ground, muffling the sound of your footsteps. Approaching the shelter, you hear voices.

"We refuse to wait any longer," a man's heavily accented voice says. "The article has been written. If you don't keep your end of the bargain, I'll see that it gets published in newspapers across the country."

You and Hannah sneak closer to the shelter to better eavesdrop on the conversation inside.

Turn to the next page.

52

"I told you, Lee Wa, I'll give it to you," Aunt Lydia says nervously. "But when I hand it over, I want the article and all the drafts. So help me, Lee Wa, if any of this leaks out I'll—"

"I don't think you're in a position to threaten me, Miss Lydia," Lee Wa replies. "I'll be waiting for you tomorrow at noon at 656 South King, in Chinatown. If I were you, I wouldn't be late."

Lee Wa goes back to his speedboat and heads out into the strait. Aunt Lydia watches him for a minute, heaves a deep sigh, and returns to her boat.

After she leaves, Hannah asks you, "What was that about?"

"I'm not sure," you reply, "but I think Aunt Lydia's in a lot of trouble. Something about the name 'Lee Wa' rings a bell."

"Maybe we should follow him," Hannah says. "If we can find out why he's blackmailing Aunt Lydia, we might be able to help."

"We'd better hurry, then," you say. "He's got a five-minute head start."

Back in your motorboat, you steer southeast toward Seattle. You push the throttle to the limit and keep your eye on the lights of the speedboat in the distance. Slowly the Seattle skyline comes into view on the horizon. An hour later you dock at Pier 52, just west of Chinatown.

Turn to page 62.

Unable to resist the chance to follow the light, you steer the boat through the cave's winding tunnels. The light remains in front of you, always just out of reach.

"Let's swim after it," Hannah suggests. You lower your hand into the cave water. Surprisingly, it's invitingly warm. "Okay," you agree. After fastening the boat to a large stalagmite in a protected cove, you climb into your diving suits, strap on your regulators and tanks, and plunge in.

The light seems to be coming from behind, above and below a large rock. You and Hannah swim silently after it. When you come around to the other side of the rock, a large, cavernous lagoon looms before you. You let out a low gasp of surprise.

Green spotlights swirl over the rocks, casting an eerie glow. Toward the rear a U-Boat Worx miniature submarine circles, its periscope rotating slowly.

You and Hannah scurry behind a rock ledge to better observe the activity. Overhead, a steel catwalk connects two small towers. Several burly men in white lab coats with clipboards are gathered together. They seem to be discussing the sub's movements. So far you haven't been spotted.

Turn to page 60.

54

At dawn you realize the mystery ship is anchored over the wreck.

Jumping into the motorboat, you throw the throttle forward and race as fast as possible toward the vessel. At 300 yards you realize it's not a fishing boat at all—it's a ship flying a pirate flag!

"What now?" Hannah asks. You know her tone all too well. She is both frightened and fighting mad.

"We'd better start diving. If we don't, they'll get everything," you say.

You suit up and slip overboard. Hannah hooks the waterproof LED screen and echo probe onto her belt before joining you.

Turn to page 56.

56

Together you swim down into the black water, confident no one has seen you—yet. Your body is tense, searching for signs of the pirates.

Suddenly Hannah stops moving and points to her right. There's activity in the distance. It's too far away to tell what it is. It could be a large school of sockeye salmon swimming by. It could be a giant squid slithering along the bottom. Or it could be a minisub looting the treasure of the *Onyx Dragon*.

Hannah aims the sonic probe toward the activity. Your fears are confirmed. The LED screen shows the clear outline of a minisub. Five divers are swimming around it.

Slowly you swim toward the *Onyx Dragon*. When you are close, you take refuge behind a rock ledge. The stern of the sunken ship is in front of you, shielding you and Hannah from the other divers. The wooden skeletal remains of the ship seem fragile in the strong current.

When it looks safe, Hannah quickly dives to the sandy bottom and begins digging. Keeping a suspicious eye toward the divers, you swim down to join her. You dig through the silky sand, sifting it through your fingers, looking for coins.

Within minutes you have uncovered dozens of large gold coins. As you sift, Hannah loads the coins into her goodie bag. Once the bag is full, she points toward the surface and swims away. You nod and continue the harvest.

Go on to the next page.

After your bag is filled, you start swimming toward the surface. You don't think the pirates have seen you, but you can't be sure. Hannah has taken the sonic probe with her, so you swim slowly, trying not to arouse suspicion or kick up too much silty sand in your wake.

Just when you think you're safe, a large hand grabs your ankle in a steely grip. You look down in panic. A pirate diver has you in his clutches. Quickly you flick off his mask with your free foot. The diver momentarily releases his grip, and you scramble toward the surface.

Hannah is in the boat, the engine running. As you are climbing aboard, the diver's hand grabs you about the waist. Spitting out your regulator, you scream for help. Hannah hurls herself onto the pirate's back. With incredible swiftness he lets go of you, grabs Hannah around the neck, and begins swimming toward the pirate ship. You watch in horror as your sister, kicking and screaming, is towed away.

Turn to the next page.

58

It won't be long before the other pirates come after you. You have to act fast. Surprise is your best defense.

You gently steer your boat over to the pirate ship and grab on to a line hanging off the port side. Tucking a flare gun into your waistband, you tie off your boat, climb on board the ship, and duck into the first open hatch you see.

Ten bunk beds line the walls. The smell of sweat, dirt, and decay is overpowering. In the corner, a huge rat is gnawing at what looks like a bone. Slowly you enter the next cabin.

This one is completely different. There are Oriental carpets on the floor, and the air smells heady of sandalwood and musk. It must be the ringleader's cabin. A perfect place to hide the treasure.

Sure enough, a little snooping around reveals the pirates' haul in the ammunition chest at the foot of the bunk. You let out a gasp as you open it—it's full of shiny gold coins, precious gems, and sparkling diamonds.

Go on to the next page.

Before you start to stuff your pockets with the treasure, you remember it's not the goods you're after, it's Hannah. You stuff a dozen of the coins into your pocket and continue your search of the cabins. So far your luck is holding out—none of the crew is on board. They must be out diving for more gold, or looking for you elsewhere.

Your heart jumps when you find Hannah, bound and gagged, lying on a dirty cot at the end of the hall. Raising a finger to your lips, you stealthily creep into the room, untie your sister, and silently motion toward the door.

"We'd better hurry," Hannah tells you in a choking whisper. "The guard just headed off to the bridge."

Together you scramble down the hall. As you approach the captain's cabin, you pause. It would be so easy to sneak in and take the treasure. The thought is unbelievably tempting—but are those footsteps approaching nearby?

If you decide to steal the treasure before escaping, turn to page 81.

If you decide to continue your escape, turn to page 94.

"What is this place?" Hannah whispers. Her voice is filled with disbelief. "And those people overhead—what strange accents."

"Shhh," you hiss. "Listen. They're talking about the sub's radar capabilities."

Motioning Hannah to your left, you swim a safe distance from the lagoon and crawl up onto a flat rock.

"Something very strange is going on in here," Hannah says fearfully. "I mean, what are these people doing in a cave in the middle of the San Juan Islands? It makes no sense."

"It makes perfect sense," you reply glumly. "This is a very strategic location. Think about it— the Bangor nuclear sub base is 70 miles to the south. And Boeing, the aerospace giant, is in downtown Seattle. Vancouver, B.C. is only 60 miles to the north. They have one of the most sophisticated electromagnetic labs in the world. This would be a perfect place for a spy base."

"What do we do now?" Hannah moans.

"The way I see it, we have two options," you answer. "We can head back and contact the authorities. Or we can do a little investigating on our own and see if our suspicions are right."

If you choose to head back to shore, turn to page 96.

If you choose to investigate, turn to page 101.

62

You and Hannah are familiar with Chinatown from past visits. You race up the pier past the Wing Luke Museum, heading toward the Danny Woo International District Gardens. As you round the corner of Maynard and King you see Lee Wa standing near an arched doorway. Above the door is a discreet sign. Lee Wa disappears inside.

"Let's follow him," Hannah says.

"Not so fast," you reply. "We don't want him to know he's being tailed." You steer your sister into the Jade Garden restaurant across the street from the building. Suddenly you realize you are starving. You take a booth next to the window and order hot and sour soup, spring rolls, and crab with black bean sauce.

"Can you see what the brass plate above the doorway says, Hannah?" you ask, slurping your soup.

"Well, let's see. It says...the Shi-Wa Family Association," Hannah replies.

"Shi-Wa!" you exclaim. "No wonder that name sounded so familiar. That's the name of the family that chartered the *Onyx Dragon* in 1852. It must mean that Lee Wa has something on Aunt Lydia."

"I can't imagine what," Hannah says. "But I think we should do a little investigating before tomorrow's meeting."

Turn to page 64.

64

A few minutes later you see Lee Wa leave the building. You quickly pay your tab, cross the street, and enter the Shi-Wa building. As you approach the front desk, you can't help but notice the decor. The walls are covered with red silk, faded from the sunlight. From them hang exotic Chinese wood-block prints of country scenes. The carpet is forest green. The scent of jasmine incense hangs heavy in the air.

A small Chinese man in a dark suit sits behind the desk, regarding you impassively. As soon as you ask about Lee Wa, the man's face goes pale. "One moment, please. I will get someone to help you." He quickly disappears behind a heavy black velvet curtain.

He returns a minute later with two burly men at his side. One of the men grabs your arm. "Please follow me," he growls. There's nothing polite about his request.

The man leads you and Hannah into a small room. Here the walls are covered with shiny gold patterned fabric. An ornate gilded throne takes up most of the room. Upon the throne is an elegant woman, seated with perfect posture. She is dressed in a long red silk robe trimmed in gold. Her fingers are adorned with emerald and ruby rings, and around her neck is a choker of diamonds.

She scrutinizes you closely before speaking. "What do you want with Lee Wa?" she asks in a stern tone.

Turn to page 66.

"We just wanted to ask him some questions," you reply quietly. "We don't want to cause him any trouble."

"You cause him trouble? Ha!" the woman laughs scornfully. "That boy has been nothing but trouble since the day he was born." She leans forward and peers at you. "I am his Auntie Shin-Wa. I am head of the Shi-Wa Family Association.

"You can trust me," she continues in a hushed tone. "Now tell me, why do you really want to see Lee Wa?"

If you decide to trust Shin-Wa, turn to page 77.

If you feel you should not trust her, turn to page 82.

"Aunt Lydia can wait," you say to Hannah. "These lights appear only once a year. I want to find out what they are."

You keep a steady course toward the distant lights. Their strange orange glow reminds you of fireflies flickering in the night. You push the throttle forward, hoping to catch up with them.

"They seem to be heading toward Iceberg Point on Lopez Island," Hannah says.

The lights become bigger and brighter as you draw closer. The full moon casts an eerie silver glow over the scene. The cool night air whistles past your ears.

"They look like they're on Lopez Island," you say. "Let's go ashore and follow them on foot."

"Wait!" Hannah cries. "Look behind us!"

Looking back, you see a dense cloud of fog swirling over the water. It looks almost like a storm—except that the rest of the night sky is clear.

If you wish to investigate the lights on the island, turn to the next page.

If you turn around to investigate the fog, turn to page 75.

68

"We came to check out the reports of mysterious lights, and that's what we're going to do, " you tell Hannah.

The boat rides the waves up onto a sandy beach on Lopez Island. After you and Hannah have secured your vessel, you set off toward the lights now flickering in the woods.

As you creep through the dark forest, you hear a rhythmic chant. It becomes louder and louder as you approach and then stops altogether.

"This is kind of spooky," Hannah whispers.

Beyond a small grove of fir trees, you see a wide circle of light. You grab Hannah's arm and gesture for her to climb onto the low branch of a poplar tree for a better view.

From your vantage you can see a clearing. Eight Indians stand around a small fire, their arms pointed toward the sky. They wear deerskin chaps on their legs, and their chests are painted with bright yellow stripes shaped like arrows. On their heads are black headbands with eagle feathers dyed red, orange, and blue. In the center of their headbands is a carved disk that looks like a small shell.

Behind them, a dozen more tribe members gaze intently out toward the Olympic Mountains to the south. They shake gourds filled with seeds and beat furiously on deerskin drums. Several torches burn brightly along the shore.

Go on to the next page.

"This must be some sacred ceremony," Hannah whispers. "Look at all their—" Just then the branch you're sitting on snaps in half. With a loud crash you and Hannah tumble to the ground. When you look up, several faces are glaring back at you in anger.

"We're—I'm sorry," you begin. "We saw the lights and I thought you wouldn't mind if—"

At first the Indians say nothing. Then the tallest one speaks. "You have interrupted our Halaayt ceremony," he says. "This is a sacred ceremony we perform only once a year." The Indians continue to stare at you. Their penetrating gaze is frightening.

"I'm really sorry," you say again. "We didn't mean any harm."

The tall Indian looks toward the moon, then back at you. "We will allow you to watch the remainder of our ceremony. But you must never tell anyone what you have seen. We have kept our ceremony private so as not to disturb the spirit we worship. It is important that the knowledge of this spirit remains only with our people."

After you agree, he motions to the ground and sits next to you. As the ceremony resumes, he tells you in a low voice, "We are members of the Kwakiutl tribe of the Tsimshian Indians. My name is Gunnahho. This ceremony marks the arrival of the Sun-Salmon to our waters."

Turn to the next page.

"The Sun-Salmon?" you whisper. Before you, the eight dancers resume their chanting. Slowly they circle the fire, arms linked.

"Many years ago, in another time, there was an Indian who descended from the sun to the Earth," Gunnahho begins. "The sun-man befriended a salmon, who was known for his powers of rejuvenation. The salmon and the sun-man became good friends. They spent many days together on the land.

"One day the salmon knew it was time to return to the water. He had been granted the power to live on land for a year, but the year was over. Because the salmon did not want to be separated from his good friend, he convinced the sun-man to become a fish like him.

"At first the sun-man hesitated," Gunnahho continues. "Because he was such a good fisherman, he held a position of great importance in the tribes. He could paddle out in his canoe, put his face to the water, and hundreds of fish would surface, drawn to the light. If he were to leave the tribe they would lose a great provider of food."

Gunnahho pauses for a moment, watching the dancers circle the fire. "In the end, the sun-man missed his friend the salmon too much. He decided to become a fish. But even after the sun-man became a salmon, he continued to provide his friends and family back on land with bountiful catches. In thanks, the Indians built a bridge of arrows for the Sun-Salmon to crawl back to land on—if he should ever miss being a man."

Turn to page 72.

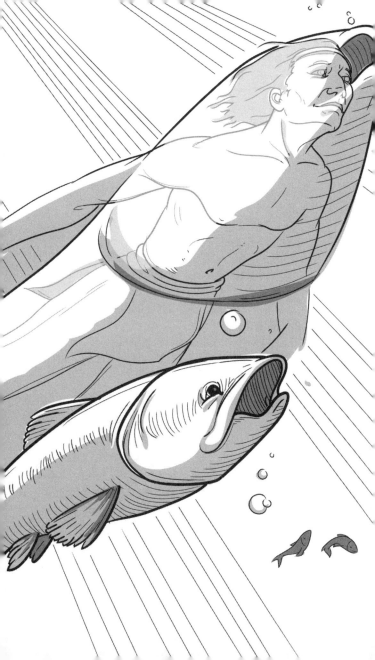

You listen intently, watching the Indians dance in the hazy smoke of the fire. Gunnahho continues, "The sun-man likes the ocean so much he returns to land only once a year—tonight. When he comes, he brings small treasures to offer us. They are collected by the young boys in the tribe and brought to land in torchlight canoes."

Gunnahho stands up and gazes toward the distance. "Here come the canoes now."

Eight wooden canoes drift into shore. Bright torches burn in their bows. As Gunnahho greets them, one young Indian boy thrusts his cupped hands forward. You peer over Gunnahho's shoulder for a better look. He holds five gold coins bearing the imprint of a Chinese ruler. All the young boys smile.

"They're the coins from the *Onyx Dragon!*" you whisper back to Hannah. Your sister stares in amazement.

Turn to page 129.

The sky turns from gray to purple to deep blue, then stars begin to appear. A full moon rises from the east. Surveying the horizon, you see nothing.

Suddenly Hannah calls out, "Look, over there, in the distance—a glow."

On the far horizon you spot them. Ten, twenty, thirty glowing lights are slowly moving toward you. They are bright orange and oval shaped. A shiver runs down your spine.

As you stare silently at the approaching lights, you hear a droning sound. You turn to the north and see a small boat heading toward the bay. The light of the moon illuminates the driver's face.

"It's Aunt Lydia!" you gasp in surprise. "She must have borrowed a boat from Zoot at the dive shop. What on earth is she doing here?"

The mysterious glowing lights begin to move to the south. You wonder if you should follow them or follow Aunt Lydia's boat.

If you follow Aunt Lydia's boat,
turn to page 51.

If you follow the mysterious lights,
turn to page 67.

Turning the boat around, you say to Hannah, "That's the strangest thing I've ever seen—a billowing cloud of fog in the middle of the strait on a calm and cloudless night!"

You steer the boat directly into the dense fog. At first all is eerily quiet. You can't see a thing through the dense haze. But then you think you hear voices in the distance.

Cautiously you move forward through the fog toward the voices. The water becomes choppier, and soon you are being tossed by ten-foot swells.

"Look! Over there!" Hannah cries, pointing.

You can hardly believe your eyes. The silhouette of a five-masted sailing schooner with all sails billowing out appears less than a hundred yards away. "Hannah, do you know what that is?" you ask incredulously. "It's the *Onyx Dragon*!"

Suddenly the wind picks up and heavy drops of rain start to fall. The water becomes even rougher, tossing you back and forth like a toy boat in a bathtub. The *Onyx Dragon* is also pitching violently, caught in the storm's fierce gale.

Turn to the next page.

76

Suddenly you hear voices clearly coming from the ship. "We're going down!" a mournful male voice cries out. "We'll lose everything!"

The deck of the *Onyx Dragon* comes into sharper focus. The crew stands on board, doing everything they can to maintain their balance. You and Hannah grip the gunwale of your own boat in an attempt to steady yourselves.

A man in a uniform is on the bridge, frantically pulling at a jib line, trying to lower the mainsail. He's wearing a captain's hat. "Captain MacGregor," someone calls to him, "watch out for the boom!"

The boom swerves sharply to the left, sweeping your Great-Great-Uncle MacGregor overboard. You react instinctively, pushing the throttle of your boat forward to rescue him.

"No!" Hannah cries to you. "He's only a ghost!"

But it's too late. As you draw closer to the *Onyx Dragon*, your boat is seized by the heaving swells. You lose your grip on the wheel. As your motor rises above the water line, the boat jerks sharply to the right, and you and Hannah are thrown head over heels into the churning, icy water. It's too late—soon you will join Captain MacGregor on the bottom of the strait.

The End

Silently you gaze at Shin-Wa. Her black eyes are soft and friendly. Glancing toward Hannah, you can tell your sister also believes Shin-Wa is trustworthy.

"The reason we wanted to see Lee Wa is because he's blackmailing our aunt—and we want to know why," you blurt out.

At the mention of the word 'blackmail,' Shin-Wa's eyes open wide. "Blackmail!" she wails. "I feared his promise to reform was too good to be true."

She pauses before continuing. "Lee Wa was my sister's only child. She died during childbirth, and Lee Wa was raised by many different relatives over the years. But no one could control him—he was a wild child. When Lee became involved in the Chinese underground, the family had no choice. He was expelled from the association for five years. We hoped that he would reform. But I can see now that it has done no good. He's up to his old tricks again," Shin-Wa says, shaking her head sadly.

You quickly fill Shin-Wa in on the secret meeting you saw at the cove and your Great-Great-Uncle MacGregor's connection to Aunt Lydia. "We must intervene," Shin-Wa says when you finish. "Lee Wa was just here. He asked for an appointment tomorrow to plead his case for reinstatement. Now I can see that he is using this place as a cover for his activities."

Turn to the next page.

78

Shin-Wa pauses thoughtfully. "You two shall be my guests overnight in a suite upstairs," she says. "We'll let Lee Wa meet your aunt here tomorrow as expected—except that a few uninvited guests will be here as well. I'll handle everything. And thank you for trusting me."

Your suite is four rooms on the top floor. They are beautifully decorated with flowers, scented candles, and more exotic Chinese prints. You lie down on the softest feather bed imaginable, and it is only a matter of moments before you are sound asleep.

The next morning you wait impatiently for the meeting to take place. Shin-Wa has arranged for you and Hannah to hide with two Seattle policemen on the balcony above the throne room. At exactly noon, Lee Wa and Aunt Lydia enter the room.

"I brought it with me," Aunt Lydia says nervously, clutching an envelope in her hand. "Now I want the article and the drafts. Please."

"Not so fast," Lee Wa says, grabbing the envelope. "You've given up the deed to half the property on San Juan, but I've changed my mind. I want the other half as well. And a little cash, too. After all, you have a pretty big family secret to hide."

Your aunt gasps. Just then a policeman hidden behind the throne jumps out and yells, "Freeze!" You run downstairs with the two policemen and join in Lee Wa's arrest. He is handcuffed and dragged away.

Go on to the next page.

"What on earth are you two doing here?" Aunt Lydia asks with surprise when she sees you.

"We could ask the same of you," you reply. "After all, you're supposed to be in New York." You introduce Shin-Wa and quickly explain her part in the whole operation. "Tell us, Aunt Lydia— what is this big family secret you're hiding? You do kind of owe us an explanation."

"I was hoping you'd never have to find this out," Aunt Lydia says quietly. "But I guess it is time for Shin-Wa to get a chance to hear this, too. When the *Onyx Dragon* went down in 1852, she was carrying the Shi-Wa family treasure. But it wasn't lost on the bottom of Puget Sound as everyone thought. MacGregor's twin brother, Sean, recovered most of the treasure and sold it on the black market to pay off his gambling debts. He also used it to buy the property on San Juan Island, as well as family mansions in Seattle and New York. Those houses are long gone now—but the property on San Juan remains. I didn't want to give it up." Aunt Lydia lowers her head in shame.

"That explains the article in the telescope," you say to Hannah. "The diamond necklace spotted on that woman's neck was stolen property."

"That's also why your father stopped looking for the *Onyx Dragon*," Aunt Lydia says. "Once I explained the secret to him, he thought it was best to abandon his search."

Turn to the next page.

Aunt Lydia turns to Shin-Wa and says respectfully, "I know you are the granddaughter of the late empress Shi-Wa. Although I can't undo the deeds of my past relatives, I would like to make restitution to your family for my Uncle Sean's shameful actions. I would like to offer you the deed to half the property on San Juan. You may do with it as you see fit."

"That is a most generous offer," Shin-Wa says quietly. She smiles at Aunt Lydia before continuing, "The Shi-Wa Association has wanted to build a family compound for some time now, but we could not afford to buy any land. You see, my family lost most of its wealth during the Cultural Revolution in China."

Shin-Wa pauses for a moment. "I accept your gracious offer," she says finally. "Our association will build a compound on the property as soon as we can raise the funds for construction."

She smiles softly, looking from Hannah to Aunt Lydia to you. "There is one condition though—on our first Chinese New Year's in the compound, all of you must be our guests at a banquet in your honor."

You turn and smile at Hannah. "That's one party I won't miss!"

The End

You point toward the captain's cabin and quietly open the door. The interior is darker than you remember. You pull Hannah inside with you as the footsteps go past the door and down the hall.

"Are you out of your mind?" Hannah whispers angrily. "These guys aren't your average sailors, you know. They're pirates!"

"Trust me," you reply.

Looking around the room, you notice the curtains have been drawn. Someone has been here between the time you saw the treasure and rescued Hannah! Realizing you have no time to spare, you head for the cache.

Suddenly the room is filled with bright light. "Looking for this?" a tall man with a deep accent says. He's blocking the door. In his large hands he holds some gold coins. His smile is sinister, and you notice there are diamonds embedded in his two front teeth.

"Uh, no," you begin, trying to think of something to say. "We were—I was—ummm…looking for a way back to my boat."

His smile turns into a frown. "You disappoint me," he says. "Somehow I thought you'd come up with something more clever than that." He tosses the coins on to the bed and quickly pulls a knife out of a sheath strapped to his ankle.

Turn to page 88.

Anyone related to Lee Wa can't be trusted, you think to yourself. "Really, we just wanted to ask him some questions," you say casually to Shin-Wa. "Nothing important. We'll try to catch up with him another time." You and Hannah scurry toward the door.

Back on the street you discuss your next move. "Maybe we should make a few discreet inquiries in the local restaurants," you say. "Someone might know where he lives. We could then pay him a surprise visit."

Hannah agrees, and together you stroll into a crowded restaurant named House of Hong one block north. Waiters zoom by with steaming carts of dim sum. Finally you catch the hostess's eye.

"Party of two?" she asks impatiently.

"Actually we're here looking for a—friend," you say. "Maybe you've heard of him—Lee Wa?"

The woman glances nervously over her shoulder. "Sure, I know him," she says. She stares at you silently, then smiles. "Wait ten minutes. I'll take you over to his gambling club when I go on break." She disappears into the kitchen.

Fifteen minutes later you are standing with the woman and Hannah in a dark alley, looking for the club entrance. "I can't believe a club would be in such a dark place," Hannah says nervously. "I think maybe we just better head back."

"Not so fast," a man behind you says. You recognize Lee Wa's voice. "Who are you? What do you want with me?"

Go on to the next page.

"Lydia is our aunt," Hannah says defiantly.

"Oh, she is, is she?" Lee Wa says with a sinister smile. "Well, prepare for a little voyage. I don't need the two of you around tomorrow to mess things up." He turns toward the woman. "Song, see that these two get packed on board the ship to Shanghai. We're leaving tomorrow afternoon, and I want them out of the way."

You turn to run. Lee Wa grabs your wrist and covers your mouth with a cloth. It smells sickly sweet. A second before you pass out you realize it's ether.

You wake up seated in a chair, your hands tightly bound behind your back. You have a pounding headache. You listen for a moment. Judging by the sound of the powerful engines below, you are on a freight ship.

The room has a small porthole. As your eyes adjust to the light, you spot Hannah tied to a chair ten feet away. You slowly rock your chair toward her.

Turn to the next page.

84

"Hannah, sit still," you say as she awakens. "I'm going to try to untie the ropes binding your hands." After half an hour of struggle, you finally manage to free your sister's hands. She quickly does the same for you.

You both rush to the porthole. There are no landmarks—only water. "We must be in the middle of the ocean," Hannah says fearfully.

Glancing down, you see a lifeboat on deck. "That's our only hope for escape," you say, pointing toward the small craft. "We have to get off this ship."

"Maybe we should just wait until we get to Shanghai," Hannah says. "We have no supplies, no nautical charts, no radio or satellite or…"

"Hannah, there's no guarantee they won't throw us overboard before we even get to Shanghai," you say. But you have to admit your sister has a point.

"Listen," you continue. "I have my cell phone with a GPS app. The battery is over half full. It should be enough."

If you change your mind and decide to wait, turn to page 123.

If you decide your best hope is to escape now, turn to page 127.

"I say we follow the historian's map," you say to Hannah. "I'm afraid the tribal map may have lost some accuracy after being passed down through so many generations."

You approach Nahpee. "My sister and I want to thank you for your hospitality. The tribal dances were fascinating," you say. "But after much thought, we've decided to follow the historian's map to search for the treasure." You look at Nahpee, hoping he isn't offended by your decision.

Nahpee scrutinizes you silently before speaking. "I appreciate your honesty, and I wish you luck. But I must warn you before you go." His voice becomes grave. "Last night we decided to search for the treasure—with or without your help. Our village is in need of funds for a better school and a medical clinic. The treasure could provide these things for us."

Nahpee pauses for a moment. "We know these waters well. They are very dangerous. You should proceed with great caution when searching for the *Onyx Dragon*."

As you scramble back down the mountain, you silently repeat Nahpee's words over and over again in your mind. "You know," you call back to Hannah, "I wonder if Nahpee was saying those things to scare us away. Won't he be surprised when we discover the treasure first!"

Turn to the next page.

Back at Aunt Lydia's house, you quickly reload your backpacks with food and diving supplies and set off in her motorboat to search for the *Onyx Dragon*. An hour later you locate the general area where the historian's map indicates the ship sank. Together you and Hannah slowly crawl into your pyrostretch neoprene jumpsuits, strap on your tanks and regulators, and back roll overboard into the dark, inky waters below.

The plunge into the cold, dark water is a shock. Your heart rate underwater is double that on land. You concentrate on breathing, trying not to hyperventilate. Peering through your mask, you watch a large school of coho salmon swim by.

Then something overhead catches your eye. Looking up, you see a large boat circle above. From its size and shape, you think it must be a Cigarette—the superfast boat favored by smugglers around the world.

As the Cigarette idles, three divers plunge into the water. They swim toward you, large netted bags dangling from their belts. Grabbing Hannah's arm, you dive to a depth where you know you'll be invisible. You point to a large crevice in a rock below you. You and Hannah wedge your bodies into the narrow space and hide.

Go on to the next page.

The divers swim by. They seem to know what they're doing. Together they roll a large boulder away from the mouth of an underwater cave. One diver disappears into the cave, then begins handing out goodie bags loaded with small green bricks. Once their bags are full, the divers head toward the surface. You and Hannah wait until their Cigarette is gone before beginning your ascent.

You climb back into your boat only to discover your engine cover has been pried off. The connector wire is cut, and your spark plugs are gone. "Great," you say in disgust. You find a spare pair of plugs in the emergency kit and begin splicing the connector wires back together.

"Who were those guys?" Hannah asks. "And what were those strange green things they pulled from the cave?"

"I don't know," you say, "but I'd certainly like to find out." In the distance you can see the Cigarette speeding away.

"It looks like they're heading for Shaw Island," Hannah says. "Maybe we should follow them."

If you want to follow the Cigarette, turn to page 106.

If you want to resume diving, turn to page 111.

You reach for your flare gun, but he kicks it out of your hand. In a flash, he grabs you and Hannah by the arms. Locked in his tight grip, he drags you up to the ship's deck.

"No!" you yell. "You can take me, but leave Hannah alone!"

The man laughs until his face turns beet red. "Leave her alone! You have no power here. Seadog!" he barks to a small man with a weasel face. "Dispose of these two!" He pushes the two of you forward. You can't believe this is happening!

Seadog smiles with obvious pleasure. He binds your hands together behind your back with thick plastic ties, blindfolds you, and shoves you toward the bow.

"The gangplank for both of you!" he yells merrily. You hear a loud splash as Hannah is pushed overboard. You let out a little yelp of fear. Seadog laughs and nudges you forward. The ice cold water rushes up. In seconds you begin to sink.

The End

"Nootka told me an old Coast Salish saying— listen to the depths of your heart, and your reward will follow," you say to Hannah. "What it means is that if we listen to the story and follow its course, we'll be rewarded. Come on!"

You pack quickly and find Nahpee in his shack. "We're heading out to find the *Onyx Dragon*. I just wanted to thank you for everything. I promise we'll be back as soon as we discover anything. Wish us luck."

"I'll wish you more than luck," Nahpee tells you in a serious tone. "I'm giving you a black bear's tooth. It belonged to Nu-la-kin-nah, a supernatural being who descended from the sky to spend his life at the bottom of the water. It will protect you."

You thank Nahpee for his gift and head down Mount Dallas. Back at the house, you plead your case to Aunt Lydia.

"We'll need to borrow the boat," you say quickly after filling her in on the events of last night. "And last year old Zoot promised to give us a deal on scuba gear from his shop. I'm sure his promise is still good." You look at your aunt's worried face. "Remember, Aunt Lydia, both Hannah and I are still C-card certified in diving from our lessons a few years ago. I think you can trust us on this one."

"Okay, okay," Aunt Lydia says reluctantly. "I can see I'm outnumbered here. Just use your common sense and stay out of trouble." She puts on a straw hat and heads out to her rose garden.

Turn to the next page.

You and Hannah load the boat with gear, a cooler filled with drinks, and your favorite Dungeness crab sandwiches. You fill the gas tank at the dock, and make a quick stop at Zoot's to stock up on cold-water diving gear. "More than happy to help," Old Zoot says cheerfully. "The water will be extremely cold out there, so let's see..."

He moves quickly, working off a checklist as he puts gear on the counter. "Two pyrostretch neoprene jumpsuits, Atomic dive rigging with eccoair tanks and flex valves, dice compasses, headlamps, split fins, subframe masks, titanium knives, weight belts..." The list goes on for quite a while. "No need to pay me now," he says. "I'll run a tab." You thank him as you head off.

You navigate the boat to the exact spot where Mountain Spirit saw the *Onyx Dragon* go down. Hannah tosses the anchor overboard while you do a final pre-dive check of your air reserve and regulators. Strapped into your neoprene jumpsuits, the two of you lower yourselves over the side.

At first the water feels pitch black, icy cold, and dangerous. You can't see anything. Once you begin to adjust to the temperature and darkness, you are amazed at the beauty surrounding you. Large red sockeye salmon swim by, heading back to their mountain rivers to spawn. Fields of blue-green kelp sway gracefully in the currents. Even with Hannah next to you, you feel completely alone in this exotic world.

Turn to page 93.

You begin measuring your descent by the amount of sunlight penetrating the water. Light will penetrate down to 650 feet. Past that there's little plant life. At 2,000 feet it's completely black. You guess you're about 150 feet down.

Suddenly you realize that you are no longer moving under your own power. You look around for Hannah, but she's nowhere in sight. You are being carried away from her in a strong current—and fast!

Swirling water surrounds you. You can tell by the patterns of seaweed floating by that you have plunged into a rip current. A strong underwater drag is quickly towing you south.

You know rip currents can travel at speeds up to 8 miles per hour. Two summers of scuba diving lessons have taught you what to do. You start swimming sideways to the current, hoping to break out of its ferocious grip.

But you can't break free. The water tightens its powerful grasp, dragging you out into open water against your will.

Fighting the current is draining your strength. If you surface now, you may never find the treasure. But if you continue diving downward, you might be dragged out into the ocean's murky depths, permanently.

If you decide to fight the current and continue diving, turn to page 115.

If you choose to surface to try to escape the current, turn to page 117.

94

"No time to spare," you whisper, pushing Hannah past the cabin with the gold and into the crew's quarters. The footsteps march past you down the hall.

Something large and furry slithers past your ankle. You swallow hard, trying not to scream. "We'd better hurry," Hannah whispers, grabbing your arm. "I bet the guy watching me has spotted our boat and gone to get help."

You motion toward the porthole. Using your clasped hands as a booster, you lift Hannah so she can squirm out. Once she is safely sliding down the rope, you pull yourself up out of the window and follow her.

You reach the boat and throw the throttle forward. As you speed away, a man appears on deck above you. He starts shouting and trains a submachine gun on you. Blindly, you fire your flare gun in his direction. The flare goes down the exhaust stack of the ship!

"Cover your head!" you yell to Hannah. "I think she's going to blow!"

Go on to the next page.

An enormous explosion rocks the pirate ship. Splintered pieces of wood and fiberglass shower down upon your heads. You come about and watch silently with Hannah as the remainder of the ship bursts into flames and begins to sink.

"I wonder if Aunt Lydia will believe us when we tell her we blew up a pirate ship," Hannah says quietly.

"She will when we come back with her to dive for all the treasure left on board—and for the *Onyx Dragon*," you answer with a smile on your face.

The End

Hannah nods when you say, "I guess it would be smarter to get out of here now. These people won't be very hospitable if they catch us."

You swim back to your boat, remove your diving gear, and slowly steer back toward the opening of the cave. You are careful not to make any noise. The last thing you want is to be discovered.

As you emerge from the mouth of the cave, two frogmen in slick black wet suits leap from above into your boat. Before you even have a chance to scream, one of the men puts a clammy hand over your mouth and pins your right arm behind your back. You make a muffled attempt to yell, but nothing comes out. You watch in fright as the other frogman covers Hannah's mouth with one hand and grabs the boat's throttle with the other. He quickly steers your boat away from the cave's opening. Fearful of their strength, you sit still, waiting to make your move.

When you're a safe distance from the cave, the taller frogman releases you and says, "I'm really sorry we had to do that, but it was for your own safety."

Go on to the next page.

"You're Americans!" you say in wonder. "I thought you might be part of—"

"Part of the group inside the cave?" the stockier of the two frogmen asks. "Hardly. We're Navy Seals, Spec Warfare Operatives. We're here on a reconnaissance mission, monitoring the activities of the organization inside that cave. We saw you enter the cave during the storm but it was too late to stop you. If we had, we would have blown our cover."

Turn to the next page.

"You mean you know what they're up to?" Hannah asks in disbelief.

"We've been monitoring their activities for over six months," the taller Seal says firmly. "The government isn't sure what they're planning, but it looks like they're going to make their move soon. And we have to be prepared."

"Maybe we can help," you offer.

"You certainly can," the stocky frogman says gruffly. "This is a top-secret mission. Whatever the two of you saw in there you have to forget. You can never mention this cave or the activities inside to anyone—ever again."

"But, we—" you begin.

"No buts about it," the tall frogman says firmly. He brings the boat near the shore of the island and prepares to dive overboard. "Now steer your boat toward home and don't look back. Ever."

The shorter one continues, "If we catch you two near this cave again," he continues, pulling his mask down and staring at you with steely gray eyes, "we will be forced to take you into secret custody. You won't be released until the operation is over. That could be years from now."

The Navy Seals jump into the water, giving your boat one last shove away from the island. You get the idea. Grabbing the wheel, you turn the boat back toward Aunt Lydia's house.

Turn to page 100.

100

"What do you think, Hannah?" you ask with excitement. "Can you imagine our friends' faces when we tell them this story?"

"Are you crazy?" Hannah replies in disbelief. "I've already forgotten everything that happened tonight."

The End

Very quietly, you motion to Hannah to follow as you swim back toward the lagoon. You surface and pause, waiting for her to catch up.

"What now?" she whispers.

You glance up. The men in the lab coats have disappeared into one of the towers. The catwalk is empty, and the U-Boat Worx is idling in the dark water.

"Swim over to that ledge," you say, pointing to the far side. "And remember, no sudden movements."

You surface by the ledge. About 200 yards away is a small fishing boat flying a pirate flag. "The sub is docked over by that boat," you whisper, pointing to your right. "I'm going to head over for a closer look. Stay here and keep watch. If anything suspicious happens, blink your underwater flashlight twice. I'll keep an eye out for the signal." You raise a finger to your lips as Hannah begins to protest.

The water is as flat as glass. You move slowly to avoid detection. Approaching the sub you hear voices inside. You surface and strain to listen. A deep baritone scolds, "You fools! How could you? We saw it on the monitor clear as day. Two intruders in wet suits entered the cave over an hour ago and they still haven't been found. You were supposed to be protecting the entrance!"

Turn to the next page.

"Well, get going!" the voice booms. "They have to be found—and soon. The longer they're in here, the more they'll discover. And I don't need to tell you what happens if they blow our cover and ruin our operation!"

Quickly, you dive underwater. You look back for Hannah's distress signal. Nothing. With extreme caution, you surface again.

You hear two splashes followed by quick footsteps walking away. After a safe interval, you glide toward the sub. No one seems to be near. The divers must have headed in the other direction. With barely a sound you lift the sub hatch and pull yourself in.

It's cool inside, and dark. You run your flashlight around the interior. A chair sits directly in front of a large control panel filled with depth gauges, LED radar screens, and speed controls. Two bright red buttons have Missile Fire written on them.

You open a narrow cabinet. A large black tube falls out. "Blueprints!" you whisper to yourself. You open the tube and partially unroll the sheets. After spending so many years on archeological digs, you've learned how to read blueprints. Yet for a moment you are confused. It seems these are blueprints for an elaborate tunnel set within a building. But the building has no windows.

Go on to the next page.

Somewhere in the back of your mind a thought begins to form. *Where have I seen this before?* you ask yourself. *There's a building near the airport without any windows...a big, black building...*

You shut your eyes to concentrate. Then you see it before you: the Boeing Military Defense Building! Your mind begins to race. These blueprints must be for a tunnel underneath the building. If they had a spy inside Boeing, he could funnel top-secret documents out and no one would ever know!

You shove the blueprints back in the plastic container, secure the waterproof seal, and take them with you as you crawl out of the escape hatch. So far your luck is holding. You remain undiscovered.

You surface next to Hannah and whisper, "There's not a moment to lose. I'll explain later. We've got to get out of here!"

Turn to page 105.

Your sister doesn't ask any questions. She quickly follows you back to the boat. Your survival instincts are in full gear, adrenaline pumping throughout your body. You manage to find your way out of the cave on the first try. Once on open water, you push the throttle forward, racing at full speed back to Aunt Lydia's.

Breathlessly you show your aunt the blueprints and explain where they came from. She wastes no time in calling her friend, Admiral Winters, at the Bangor submarine base. He contacts the local Navy Seals Warfare Ops representative. Together they race up to San Juan Island aboard an S-70B Seahawk helicopter.

"They're the real thing, all right," the admiral tells you after he's inspected the blueprints. "I don't know how you two did it, but you've saved our country's defense. And you've given us enough evidence to put this gang away for a long time."

A week later, with the gang safely behind bars, Admiral Winters watches as the president presents you and Hannah with Medals of Valor from the Navy, their highest honor. "This is great," you whisper to Hannah. "But, quite frankly, I can't wait to resume our search for the *Onyx Dragon*."

The End

106

Before you can follow the Cigarette, it takes you a few moments to finish splicing your connector wires together. "Keep those binoculars trained on that boat, Hannah. We don't want to lose sight of them," you say.

When your job is done, you rev up the engine and zoom through Upright Channel toward Shaw Island. Approaching the western shore, you reduce speed and glide onto a soft sandbar near Hick's Bay. Shaw Island is a private reserve for wealthy families. Its dense, fir-covered slopes rise dramatically from the water.

"The island was named after John Shaw, a nineteenth-century naval officer," you tell Hannah. "There are only a dozen or so homes on the island, mostly owned by his ancestors. I figure if we slowly circle the island we're bound to spot the docked Cigarette."

You glide a safe 100 yards off shore, scanning the island with your binoculars. Most of the houses are so secluded you only catch glimpses of their rooflines. You spot the Cigarette tied to a wooden dock nestled in a large cove. You continue steering down shore until you find a pine tree jutting from a waterside ledge where you can tie your boat. "I figure our best plan is to swim underwater into the cove and surface underneath the dock," you say. Hannah nods in agreement and prepares to dive.

You make it safely beneath the dock and lift your head above water. Hannah surfaces behind you. No one seems to be around. You crawl up onto the

Go on to the next page.

rocky shore and remove your flippers and other diving gear. Then, clad in your wetsuits, you silently creep toward the large house.

Nearing a window, you peek inside. Two men and a woman are examining something on a table in the center of the room. One of the men holds a knife. He is cutting through a green package. "The bricks!" you whisper to Hannah.

"This is only part of the stash," the tall man with the knife says. He has a heavy Cockney accent. "The other bags are still in the cave. Figure we can head back t'ere in an hour or so. By then t' other divers should be long gone." He chuckles quietly to himself.

"What makes you so sure they didn't see you?" the woman asks in a stern voice with a refined English accent.

"Just these little park slugs," he replies in Cockney, proudly displaying your spark plugs.

"It's important no one suspects what we're up to, Mickie," the woman continues.

"Hold your horses, duchess," the tall man cuts in. "No one suspects—just like no one has caught on to their missing household goods yet. This is a foolproof plan if there ever was one. We finish robbing the island houses tonight. Two days from now you're fencing the goods abroad. No blokes wise to the scheme and we all get rich." He chuckles again.

Turn to the next page.

108

"Which island is next on the list?" the woman asks the shorter man.

"San Juan," he replies. "Three houses altogether. Two on the south side and a tall Victorian one on the southwest bluff. We'll finish about 2 A.M. There'll be just enough time for you to catch your morning flight."

"Well, finish loading the jewelry into the bottoms of these statues," the woman says, pointing to several stone figurines on the floor. "I'll be waiting for you outside the British Airways terminal tomorrow at 7 A.M. sharp. And don't mess up or else—" She draws a long red fingernail across her throat and leaves the room.

You and Hannah scramble back toward the dock. Safely out of sight, you whisper, "Hannah, did you hear that? They're jewel thieves—and they're about to rob San Juan. Worse yet, I have a creepy feeling the Victorian one on the southwest bluff is Aunt Lydia's house!"

"What are we going to do?" Hannah asks fearfully.

You close your eyes and think for a moment. "We'll catch them in the act," you say. "Come on. I've got a plan."

By the time you get back to the house, Aunt Lydia is gone. "Look, here's a note," Hannah says.

Gone to Seattle overnight for a lecture at the university. If you need me I'll be staying at the Sorrento Hotel. Otherwise, lots of food in fridge. Have a good evening & I'll see you tomorrow around noon. Love, Aunt L.

Go on to the next page.

"Perfect," you say. "We have the house to ourselves. Now we can plan our surprise attack without having to worry about anyone getting in our way."

You and Hannah impatiently wait for the sky to darken. Because you are so far north, the sun doesn't set until nearly 10 P.M. in the summer. Finally you watch as the sun's orange glow sinks behind the snow-capped Olympic Mountains. Everything is set.

"All we need now are a couple of robbers to catch," Hannah says excitedly. "This is more fun than looking for the *Onyx Dragon!*"

You have turned off all the lights in the house. Together you sit in the dark. Every noise seems to be magnified. Crickets chirp loudly outside in the sea grass. You can hear the waves lapping the shore near the boathouse. A great horned owl hoots nearby. Finally, in the distance, you hear the distinct purr of a Cigarette engine in low gear.

"They're here," you whisper, peeking out the kitchen window. The boat slowly moves toward shore. You and Hannah slip out the back door and hide yourselves behind a stone wall above the dock.

As the Cigarette nears the boathouse, the driver cuts the engine. You peer over the wall, watching in the moonlight as two figures get out. One is tall, the other short.

"Yep, that's them," Hannah whispers.

Turn to the next page.

The men quietly creep toward the house, empty rucksacks slung over their shoulders. Once they're inside you grab Hannah's arm. "It's time for us to get to work," you say, leading her down to the Cigarette. Hannah turns on her cell phone.

Twenty minutes later, you and Hannah are back in your hiding place behind the stone wall. You hear the men's voices as they come out of the house, bulging rucksacks in their hands.

"T'was quite the haul," the tall man says in his Cockney accent. "The duchess will be most pleased. Haven't seen diamond brooches like these since I last worked Geneva," he says, laughing loudly.

"Quiet, you idiot!" the short man says. "Do you want to get caught?"

"Ya 'tis a fool," the tall man replies. "As if we'd get caught out here in the middle of—"

"Not so fast," you say, leaping from behind the stone wall. You shine your flashlight in their stunned faces.

"What the—" the tall man says. "Quick! To the boat." He and his partner race toward the dock. Jumping into the Cigarette, the tall man furiously turns the ignition key. Click! Nothing happens.

"Come on, come on," he desperately pleads. The engine refuses to start. In the distance sirens can be heard. As they come closer and closer the man cranks the Cigarette engine over and over again.

"Looking for these?" you ask. In your hand are the Cigarette's spark plugs. The flashing lights of the arriving patrol cars illuminate the scene. For a moment, the tall man looks as if he might cry.

The End

"On second thought, let's let them go," you say as the Cigarette recedes in the distance.

"What makes you so sure they won't return?" Hannah asks. "I mean what if we're down there diving and they come back and—"

"Don't get so worked up," you reply. "Whatever they were after, they got. They couldn't care less about us now. The important thing is that we continue looking for the *Onyx Dragon*." Before Hannah can protest any further, you jump overboard.

Your sister soon follows. As you approach the divers' cave, you momentarily forget about the *Onyx Dragon*. *I wonder what really was in there*, you think to yourself.

You motion Hannah over. You scribble on your underwater slate, "One look inside?"

Together you strain to dislodge the boulder covering the cave entrance. After several shoves it rolls aside. Inside it is completely dark. You point to your dive watch and hold up two fingers. Hannah looks into the dark cave, shrugs her shoulders, and follows you in. *Two minutes can't hurt*, you think.

Turn to the next page.

112

Running your flashlight around the cave floor, you are surprised to see at least a dozen more green bricks lying in the sand. You pick up one to examine it. The package is covered with green plastic held together by waterproof tape. Slitting the edges of the tape with your titanium knife, you pull a small brown box from inside the plastic. Inside are nine diamond rings, each one larger than the last.

Go on to the next page.

Suddenly a diver swims out from around the boulder and into the cave. He's heading right toward you. It's too late! There's nowhere to go. Within seconds he's upon you.

You lash at the diver with your knife, in vain. He kicks it out of your hand and trains a spear gun on you. You're frozen in terror as he fills his dive bag with the remaining green bricks and skillfully backs out of the cave. He keeps his spear gun trained on you and Hannah at all times.

Maybe he'll just take off and spare us, you hope to yourself. No such luck. As he leaves the cave, he and another diver shove the boulder back into place. You're trapped inside!

You and Hannah push at the boulder with all your might. It's no use. The rock feels like it's cemented to the opening. Exhausted, you huddle together in the dark cave.

Fifteen minutes pass. You know that if you remain underwater much longer you'll really be in trouble. You check your oxygen level. Ten minutes of air left. You need that time to decompress on your ascent.

Turn to the next page.

A heavy feeling starts to come over you. You can barely breathe. A small alarm sounds in your head. "I'm out of oxygen," you gasp to Hannah. But your sister is motionless next to you.

Suddenly you have a frightening vision, which you know will come true. Sometime in the future an explorer will roll back the boulder to discover two skeletons inside the cave—and one of them will be yours!

The End

The current is strong, but you just know you are stronger. You dive deeper and deeper, trying to break the water's tight grip. Sunlight barely penetrates down this far. The water is black and cold and terrifying. *I must be 300 feet down* you think to yourself.

The harder you fight, the less progress you make. You open your dive bag to get your depth gauge. The bear tooth Nahpee gave you is sucked out by the current and flies away into the dark depths. You begin to panic.

You reverse your direction and try to swim toward the sunlight, but you are turned around and dragged back deeper into the murky water. You lunge to your right, then to your left, all without effect. An eerie feeling comes over you.

"I'm soooo cold," you moan. You know that once you start shivering it will be almost impossible to stop. Your breathing pace triples. You furiously gasp oxygen from your regulator, trying to produce enough heat to warm your body.

Turn to the next page.

116

With every ounce of your remaining strength, you make one final, desperate effort to break free of the rip current. Furiously you pump your legs. Nothing happens. You only seem to be swimming in place. Your energy is gone, and now you're shivering uncontrollably.

Suddenly it seems easier not to make any effort at all. You stop swimming and begin to drift with the current's flow. Disoriented, you think you're in a dream. Dark fish swim by in slow motion. You are sapped of all your strength. You grow sleepier and sleepier. You see Nahpee and Hannah opening the ship's safe. You think of their celebration and quietly close your eyes—for the last time.

The End

You clutch the bear tooth Nahpee gave you tightly in your hand and fight to swim toward the surface. Finally, just as you're about to give up, the current releases you. You sprint upward, pedaling your fins with all your might.

From out of the murky depths, Hannah swims into view. With hurried motions she points toward the water's surface.

You burst above the waves, still shaking from what might have been.

"You'll never believe it!" Hannah gasps excitedly when you come into open air. "I think I found the ship's hull, way down below. I was waiting for you to help me explore the site but finally gave up. Where were you?!"

"I—never mind," you reply quickly. "Where's the ship?"

Turn to the next page.

118

"Follow me," she replies, with excitement in her voice. You pull your mask back down and dive after Hannah, hoping not to encounter the rip current again. You're in luck—apparently the tides have changed and the current has dissipated. The water is much calmer and you can swim quickly with ease.

About thirty feet down Hannah points toward a huge mass embedded near a rock ledge. Closer inspection reveals the remains of a wooden ship, splintered into many large pieces scattered over the sand. Together you search through the boat's skeletal remains. The wood looks heavy and water-logged, but when you touch it you are surprised at its smooth finish. Very little of the actual hull remains.

There must have been a huge impact where it struck the rocks above, you think to yourself. *It must have shattered as it sank.*

Behind a large barnacle-covered rock you discover a metal box, corroded but still intact. *This could be it,* you think. You turn toward Hannah and write on your underwater slate, "Here! Now!" Together you wrap your arms around it, straining to dislodge its weight. Once free, you slowly head toward the surface with your find, careful to decompress at stages in your ascent.

Go on to the next page.

"Quick! Hand me the compressor wrench," you say to Hannah after you've heaved the metal box into the boat. "A few air shots at the lock's pins and it should—" You aim the wrench tip at the hinge pins and blast them with some compressed air.

Turn to the next page.

120

The lid of the box flies open, screeching loudly as metal is pried from metal.

"Empty!" Hannah cries. "The stupid thing is empty!" She grabs the box and angrily throws it on the floor of the boat. On impact, the bottom springs open to reveal a secret compartment.

"Wow!" you say, reaching inside it. "Look at this—it's a large green rock." You examine the clear rock in your hand.

"There's a note, too," Hannah says. "It's some sort of list—'seventeen diamond necklaces; a jewel-encrusted dragon broach, twelve ruby rings; nineteen emeralds, including the Star of Asia; two hundred and seventy-three gold coins; fourteen bags of gold nuggets.'" Hannah looks at you with awe. "This means we've located the treasure!"

Go on to the next page.

"No," you remind her with disappointment, "we found the list of the treasure. Judging by the shape of the wreck below, the treasure was carried away by tides and currents long ago. All we found is this green thing." You hold the rock up to the sunlight. The light strikes its center, refracting thousands of green prisms all over the boat.

Turn to the next page.

Suddenly you realize what's in your hand. "It's the Star of Asia!" you cry. "The most famous emerald of all time! Wait until Nootka and Nahpee see this!"

You push the boat's throttle forward as far as it will go and zoom back to San Juan Island to break the news. You, Hannah, and Nahpee become instant celebrities. After you present the emerald to the Coast Salish at an elaborate ceremony, you all fly to New York to auction it off.

Due to all the pre-sale publicity the atmosphere at the auction is electric, with bids coming fast and furious from dealers all over the world—Paris, London, Shanghai, Rio, and Mumbai. When the final gavel is brought down the emerald sells for over ten times the presale estimate.

On the flight home, Nahpee tells you that your discovery has turned the fortunes of his tribe around. You smile at Hannah.

"It wasn't our discovery," you say quietly. "It was Mountain Spirit's."

The End

"Think about it," Hannah pleads. "We'd never last a week out on the ocean. We don't even know where we are."

Reluctantly you agree. "Well, we better tie ourselves up to these chairs again," you say. "We don't want to give ourselves away."

Suddenly you hear footsteps approach. You quickly arrange your chairs into their former positions and loosely tie the rope around your hands behind you. Shutting your eyes, you pretend you're asleep.

The door opens, and two figures enter. "See, I told you," a woman says. She sounds like Song. "They're still out of it. Those sedatives we gave them will keep them out for at least another twelve hours."

"You had better be right," Lee Wa says sternly. "When we pull into port tonight I don't want either one of them to be seen. Help me pack them into the banana crates. I'll try to bribe the customs officials to let them pass by unopened."

Turn to the next page.

124

Song doesn't seem to notice how loose the ropes are when she unties your hands. Squinting between your eyelashes, you watch as she maneuvers two large banana crates toward your chairs. You let your body go limp so that she and Lee Wa can pick you up and lower you into the crate.

"We should nail these shut," Lee Wa says

"No," Song says. "The latches will work just fine. Besides what if we need to dispose of our 'hidden cargo' quickly. It's easier for us."

"Good thinking," Lee Wa replies with a sinister tone. He secures the crate latches.

Slowly you open your eyes. Between the crate's wooden slats you catch a glimpse of Hannah being lowered inside her crate.

Go on to the next page.

Once Song and Lee Wa have left the room, you whisper to Hannah, "Don't say a thing until we're on the dock. We don't want to blow our cover. Then when I give the signal, make as much noise as possible."

You wait in the banana crate impatiently. It seems to take forever before you pull into port. Finally you can feel the ship slow down. Within minutes the vessel has come to a complete stop and the door opens. Two large men lift your crate and place it on a dolly. Hannah's crate is placed on top of yours, and the two of you are wheeled from the room.

Peeking between the slats you can see that you're being off-loaded onto a large dock. Chinese men dressed in short coats and worn pants swarm around the dock, unloading crates onto a conveyor belt. The belt feeds into a small building. CUSTOMS is written above the doorway in Chinese and in English.

Impatiently, you wait your turn. Finally Hannah's crate is lifted and placed on the conveyor belt. You ride several feet behind her. You pass through a small, dark tunnel and emerge into the main holding area. Lee Wa is talking to two customs officials up ahead. As you approach, their voices become clearer.

"That about does it," Lee Wa says. "These are the last two banana crates. If you'll just sign these papers I can be on my way."

Turn to the next page.

"Now!" you hiss to Hannah. With all your might, you kick your feet against the crate's wooden slats. They break in half with a loud snap, and you clamber out. Hannah begins screaming at the top of her lungs. The stunned customs officials don't even seem to notice Lee Wa running toward the exit.

"Get him," you cry. "He's trying to escape!"

Three security men grab Lee Wa and hold on to him while a customs official calls the police. As you wait for them to arrive, you tell the official how you came to be packed in a banana crate. "I'm willing to bet that a lot more of these crates contain something other than bananas," you add.

Sure enough, when the customs men open up the rest of the crates, they find everything from stolen art to smuggled jewels and drugs. Lee Wa is hauled off to the Shanghai police station, and you and Hannah are proclaimed heroes. The Chinese government presents you with a medal, and then the U.S. ambassador takes care of all the arrangements for your return to Seattle.

Before you get on the airplane, the ambassador hands you an envelope. "This was found in Lee Wa's possession. Apparently it belongs to your aunt. You might want to find out how he got it," he says discreetly.

Suddenly you remember the mysterious lights, and how you got into all of this in the first place. "There are a lot of things I'm hoping Aunt Lydia can explain," you whisper to Hannah.

The End

"I'd rather risk an escape now," you say to Hannah.

"Maybe you're right," Hannah concedes.

"Let's sneak out on deck," you say. "You keep watch while I lower the lifeboat into the water. Then we'll jump for it. We have to act fast."

You creep into the hallway. A door at the end is marked EXIT in red. Silently you open it. No one is in sight. You quickly untie the ropes securing the lifeboat to the ship. The boat is heavy and quickly plunges into the water below.

"Hurry," you whisper to Hannah. "We have to get over before we're spotted and the boat drifts away." Taking a deep breath, you jump overboard.

Turn to the next page.

You hit the water hard. It takes a second to catch your breath. Hannah is in the distance, swimming toward you. You grab hold of the lifeboat and begin paddling toward your sister. No one on the freighter seems to have noticed your escape.

You pry the battery out of your wet cell phone. You hadn't thought about it failing before your plunge into the deep. Despite your best efforts it's soaked and refuses to work.

Two days pass. You are drifting aimlessly out on the open ocean with no food or water, and both you and Hannah are beginning to feel very weak.

At dawn on the third day Hannah yells, "Look—on the horizon—I think I see a ship!"

Using every last ounce of energy, you paddle toward the speck in the distance. No matter how hard and long you paddle, the speck remains distant. Your hopes for rescue begin to fade.

Finally your energy is spent. Your body aches with exhaustion. The sun beats down on you. You barely have the strength to speak—even when Hannah points in silent terror at the two sharks beginning to circle your lifeboat. They seem to be eyeing you for their next meal. You swallow hard and wait.

The End

"How long have you been receiving these annual gifts from the Sun-Salmon?" you ask Gunnahho.

The Indian turns toward you and answers, "My great-great-grandfather received them. Before him, I'm not sure."

You and Hannah exchange a knowing look. Your search for the treasure of the *Onyx Dragon* is over. At least the riches seem to have fallen into deserving hands.

The End

ABOUT THE ARTIST

Illustrator: Gabhor Utomo was born in Indonesia. He moved to California to pursue his passion in art. He received his degree from Academy of Art University in San Francisco in spring 2003. Since graduation, he's worked as a freelance illustrator and has illustrated a number of children's books. Gabhor lives with his wife, Dina, and his twin girls in the San Francisco Bay Area.

ABOUT THE AUTHOR

Alison Gilligan grew up in New England before moving to New York City for college, work, and life (not necessarily in that order). After graduating from NYU she worked in an art auction house and advertising agency before relocating to the Pacific NW. There she helped combat international piracy for a large software company before leaving to focus on raising a family and serving on nonprofit boards dedicated to promoting literacy and combating homelessness. She currently lives with her family in Florence, Italy, where she worships at the shrines of Brunelleschi, Bronzino, and mozzarella di bufala. She continues her volunteer work with a nonprofit dedicated to restoring Florence's art treasures. Ms. Gilligan and her family spend their summers on San Juan Island, Washington.

For games, activities, and other fun stuff, or to write to Alison Gilligan, visit us online at CYOA.com

In this book....

Angry Pirates:
15

Missing Gemstones:
73

Loony Relatives:
2

Secret Clues:
7

Ghostly Apparitions:
2

Heroes of the Story:
YOU